Padma Shri Pran

Maurice Horn, the editor of World Encyclopedia of Comics, has described cartoonist PRAN as Walt Disney of India.

Entertaining generation after generation, his comics have been constant companion of all the growing youngsters providing fun and amusement through his famous characters like CHACHA CHAUDHARY, SABU, SHRIMATIJI, PINKI, BILLOO, RAMAN etc. More than 600 of his titles are selling well in the market, and numerous comic strips are regularly appearing in various newspapers. His CHACHA CHAUDHARY comics had already been adapted for a TV Serial, and ran continuously for 600 episodes on a premier channel.

Travelling widely over the globe, he delivers lectures at various International Conferences. He has also been honoured with 'People of The Year Award' by Limca Book of Records for popularizing comics. His comic book 'United We Stand' was released in 1983 by the then Prime Minister Mrs. Indira Gandhi, and is still very popular among children.

Publisher

PINKI

REAL WATCHMAN

HE'S THE WATCHMAN OF OUR COLONY.
UNCLE, WHY ARE YOU TROUBLED ?
KIDS' HOLIDAYS HAVE STARTED. THEY'RE ASKING ME TO TAKE THEM ON A PICNIC.
THAT'S GREAT ! WHY DON'T YOU TAKE THEM ?

IF I GO, WHO'LL GUARD THE COLONY ?
I'LL DO THAT FOR A DAY.
REALLY ?
THEN I'LL GO.
YOU'VE SENT HIM TO PICNIC.

NOW, HOW WILL YOU GUARD THIS PLACE?
I'VE GOT AN IDEA !
A AAH A !
BHIKHU !
I'VE BECOME A FAN OF YOUR SINGING. WILL YOU REMAIN WITH ME TODAY AND PRACTICE ?
DONE !
www.chachachaudhary.com

AA... AA !
WOW !
O AH AA !
WHAT ARE YOU DOING HERE AT THIS HOUR, PINKI ?
GUARDING THE COLONY, JHAPATJI.
TO KEEP THE THIEVES AWAY GUARD SHOUTS "STAY AWAKE". BHIKHU IS ALSO DOING THE SAME THING BY SINGING.

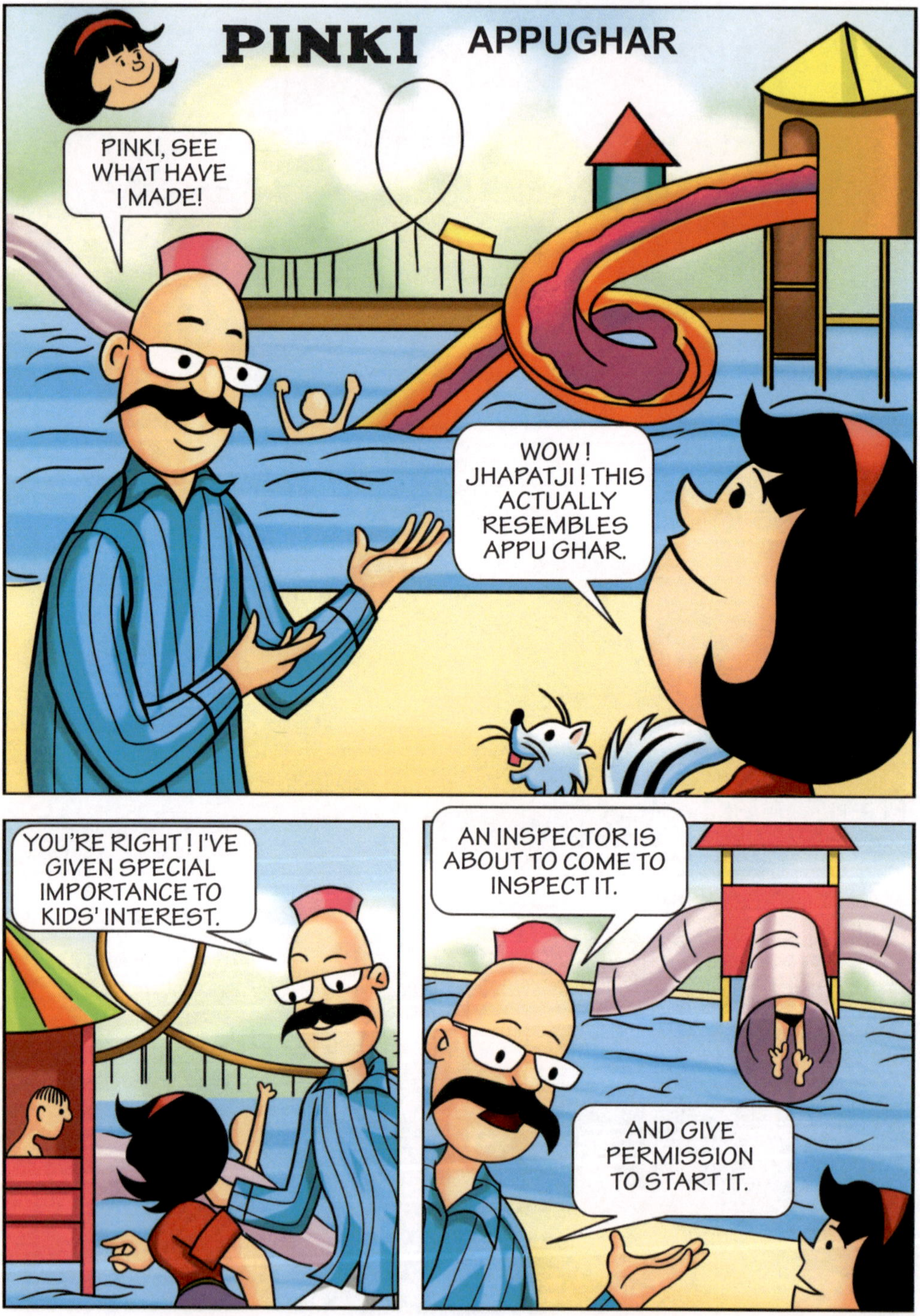
PINKI
APPUGHAR
PINKI, SEE WHAT HAVE I MADE!
WOW! JHAPATJI! THIS ACTUALLY RESEMBLES APPU GHAR.
YOU'RE RIGHT! I'VE GIVEN SPECIAL IMPORTANCE TO KIDS' INTEREST.
AN INSPECTOR IS ABOUT TO COME TO INSPECT IT.
AND GIVE PERMISSION TO START IT.

I'LL JUST ROAM AROUND TILL THEN.
WOW ! MERRY GO ROUND !
GO-ROUND.

WOW ! ITS SEAT IS WONDERFUL!
OFF
ON
CLICK!
OH ! IT HAS STARTED.
© PRAN'S FEATURES

THIS IS YOUR MISCHIEF, KUTKUT. THERE WILL BE TROUBLE IF JHAPATJI SEES IT.
SWITCH IT OFF, KUTKUT.
PLEASE KUTKUT, NO MORE MISCHIEF!
www.chachachaudhary.com

IT IS AWESOME
IS EVERYTHING READY ?
YES !
JUST NEED TO FIX THIS WIRE ON THE GIANT WHEEL. THEN EVERYTHING WILL BE FINE.
A LONG LADDER IS REQUIRED FOR FIXING THE WIRE.

LADDER ISN'T REQUIRED
MY KUTKUT WILL DO THIS FOR YOU.
PINKI ! YOU LEAVE IT.
UNCLE ! YOU CAN'T STOP ME FROM HELPING YOU.
GO, KUTKUT ! DO YOUR WORK.
© PRAN'S FEATURES

WELL DONE, KUTKUT!
GREAT LITTLE SQUIRREL! GOOD JOB!
WELL DONE!
HERE TAKE YOUR REWARD.
SQUEAK!! SQUEAK!!

SQUEAK!!
SQUEAK !!
OH!
I'LL HAVE TO DO SOMETHING FAST !!

I'M READY FOR THE INSPECTION.
JUST THEN KUTKUT SWITCHES ON THE GIANT WHEEL.
ON
OFF
GIANT WHEEL HAS STARTED RUNNING...
GIANT WHEEL IS RUNNING MORE THAN ITS SPEED.
GIANT WHEEL IS OVER SPEEDING AS KUTKUT HAS JOINED WRONG CONNECTION.
YOUR RIDES ARE OVER SPEEDING, SO YOUR PERMISSION IS CANCELLED.

Diamond TOONS
PRAN'S
CHACHA CHAUDHARY
AND
SWACHH BHARAT

CHACHA CHAUDHARY AND SWACHH BHARAT

GEETA, YOU ALSO JOIN US.
MUMMY, I AM ALSO GOING.
CAN I PLAY WITH YOUR TOY?
OF COURSE!
KIDS, DON'T MAKE ANY NOISE.
WHERE ARE WE GOING ?
TO GULZAR GARDEN.

HOW FAR IS IT ?
IT'LL TAKE HALF AN HOUR.
WOW ! WHAT A PLACE.
EVERYONE GET YOUR BAGS AND COME HERE.
MANU, LET'S PLAY FOOTBALL.
COME !

CHACHA JI, NOW IT'S TIME FOR LUNCH.
COME ON KIDS, LET'S HAVE LUNCH.
CHACHA JI, THESE KIDS HAVE LITTERED THE WHOLE PLACE.

THAT'S VERY BAD.
WHY DON'T YOU PUNISH THEM ?
NOT PUNISHMENT, BUT A LESSON.
MANU ! YOU ARE ALWAYS RIGHT. IT'S A BAD HABIT.
WHO HAS PUT THIS GARBAGE IN THE DUGDUG?
LOOK CAREFULLY. IT'S THE SAME GARBAGE WHICH YOU HAD LEFT IN THE PARK.

UFF !!
WE SHOULD HAVE DONE IT BEFORE.
YOU HAVE DIRTIED THE WHOLE PLACE.
WE SHOULD TAKE CARE OF THIS.
NOW, THEY WILL NOT LITTER ANY PLACE IN FUTURE.
COME ON KIDS, PUT THE WASTE PAPER, BOTTLES AND FOOD IN DIFFERENT COLORED BINS.

I'LL TAKE YOU TO A PLACE WHERE THIS GARBAGE IS RECYCLED THROUGH MACHINE.
WHERE CHACHA JI ?
EVERYBODY JUMP INTO DUGDUG.
PINKI, TALK LATER, FIRST COME INTO DUGDUG.
BHARAT, SHOW THEM HOW YOU RECYCLE THE GARBAGE INTO MANURE WITH THE HELP OF MACHINE.
PUT THE GARBAGE IN THE MACHINE AND START IT.
SEE, IT IS CONVERTED INTO MANURE. IT'S VERY USEFUL.

IT IS A PART OF SWACHH BHARAT ABHIYAN UNDER MINISTRY OF URBAN DEVELOPMENT .
NEVER THROW THE WASTE . USE IT IN SOME MANNER. THERE WON'T BE ANY DISEASE SPREADING AROUND.
WE'LL HAVE DOUBLE BENEFIT.
THAT'S DOUBLE USEFUL. SWACHH BHARAT ABHIYAN CAN ONLY BE SUCCESSFUL WHEN WE ALL WILL KEEP OUR AREA CLEAN.
WE ALL NEED YOUR COOPERATION.
YOU SHOULD TAKE A PLEDGE TO KEEP CLEANLINESS AROUND YOU.
WE SWACHHA GRAHI FAMILY PLEDGE TO KEEP OUR SURROUNDINGS CLEAN.

स्वच्छ भारत
एक कदम स्वच्छता की ओर
सत्यमेव जयते
Ministry of Urban Development
Government of India
कम्पोस्ट अपनाओ,
फार्म हाउस में हरियाली लाओ.
• फार्म हाउस में कम्पोस्ट का इस्तेमाल कीजिए
• ये मिट्टी को उपजाऊ बनाती है
• इसे आप नज़दीकी फर्टिलाइज़र की दुकान से खरीद सकते हैं
कम्पोस्ट बनाओ, कम्पोस्ट अपनाओ.
अधिक जानकारी के लिए
1969

PINKI
SKATE BOARDS
PAPA HAS GOT NEW SKATE BOARD.
I'LL HAVE TO LEARN USING IT.
AND YOU'LL BE ABLE TO DO SO WHEN YOU SEE HOW IT IS USED.

GIVE IT TO ME.
BUT SPORTY !!
NO IF, NO BUT. WAIT !
AND WATCH !
LOOK !
LOOK AT THIS !

BRING IT TOMORROW ALSO.
NEXT DAY-
YOU HAVE COME AT THE RIGHT TIME, PINKI. I WAS WAITING FOR YOU.
SIT AND WATCH HOW A SKATE BOARD IS USED.
www.chachachaudhary.com

COME AGAIN, PINKI.
THIS WAY I'LL NEVER LEARN TO RIDE IT.
SOB! SOB ! DO SOMETHING, KUTKUT !
WILL YOU DO SOMETHING, KUTKUT?
SQUEAK!!

GREAT !
NEXT DAY
GIVE ME YOUR SKATE BOARD.
TODAY I'LL SHOW YOU HOW TO SKATE IN FREE STYLE.
KEEP THE BOARD LIKE THIS.
AND RUN FAST LIKE THIS.
© PRAN'S FEATURES

OUCH !
CRACK!
AHHH !
BANG !
OUCH ! THIS SKATE BOARD IS USELESS.
TAKE IT AWAY… GRRR!
YOU DID A NICE JOB, KUTKUT !
OTHERWISE, I'D HAVE TO WAIT FOR DAYS TO RIDE ON IT.

PINKI FLYING BALLOON
FLYING BALLOON COMPETITION
YOU KNOW WE'RE PARTICIPATING IN THE FLYING BALLOON COMPETITION.
ISN'T IT GREAT ?
ABSOLUTELY.
SEE MY FLYING BALLOON.

SHOULD I SHOW YOU HOW IT FLIES ?
I KNOW.
SUCH BALLOONS FLY USING HOT AIR. THE HEAT EXERTS PRESSURE AT THE BOTTOM.
DUE TO THIS THE BALLOON FLIES IN THE AIR.
WOW ! YOU'RE SO AWARE, PINKI !
© PRAN'S FEATURES

AND THIS IS MY BALLOON.
OH ! SO YOU MEAN TO COMPETE WITH ME, PINKI ?
YES, YOU MAY THINK SO, SINCE YOU'RE ALSO IN THE COMPETITION.

NO ONE WILL WIN THIS COMPETITION EXCEPT ME.
LET'S SEE.
READY?
YES !!

BANG !
OFF WE GO, JHAPAT UNCLE !
NO WORRIES !! I'M SURE TO FLY HIGHER AND HIGHER.

SO CONFIDENT !
SEEMS JHAPAT UNCLE HAS COME FULLY PREPARED.
WE'VE TO WIN BY ALL MEANS.
SQUEAK!!
YOU'RE MAKING A LOT OF NOISE, KUTKUT.
YOU GO THERE AND EAT THE NUT. LET ME FOCUS ON THE RACE.

CRACK!
NOW JHAPATJI'S BALLOON WILL FLY.

UP !
ON THE
TOP.
www.chachachaudhary.com

FRRR !
FRRR !

FRRR!
FRRR!
!!
POOR JHAPATJI'S BALLOON !!
AND POOR JHAPATJI !!
GRRRR!

PINKI
RANSOM
UNCLE ! DID YOU SEE MY PET SQUIRREL, KUTKUT ?
SQUIRREL!
YES, COME WITH ME. I'LL TAKE YOU TO IT.
PINKI, YOUR SQUIRREL ENTERED THAT HOUSE.
ROBERT, I'VE LURED THE GIRL.
MY KUTKUT ISN'T HERE. YOU BEFOOLED ME.
HEY GIRL ! TELL ME YOUR PHONE NUMBER
WE DON'T HAVE A PHONE. MY UNCLE HAS IT.
TELL IT.
333325.
PEDRO ! CALL UP HER UNCLE AND ASK IF HE WILL PAY THE RANSOM OF FIVE LAKHS TO GET HIS NIECE RELEASED ?

HELLO ! WE'VE KIDNAPPED YOUR NIECE. WILL YOU PAY A RANSOM OF 5 LACS FOR HER ?
NO !
HE SAID, NO !
WARN HIM, IF THE MONEY DOESN'T REACH, WE'LL KILL HIS DAUGHTER.
WHAT ?
MY UNCLE SHOUTED SO LOUDLY THAT YOUR FRIEND'S EAR DRUM IS DAMAGED. HE'S BECOME DEAF.
OK ! I'LL TALK TO HIM.

STORES
ROBERT! WHY DID YOU BOTHER YOURSELF? I WOULD HAVE SENT THE THINGS TO YOUR HOME.
I WANT TO MAKE A CALL.
333325? ... YOU WILL KEEP RS. 5 LAC UNDER THE BANYAN TREE OTHERWISE, I'LL KILL THE GIRL. TELL ME, YES OR NO? ANSWER IN A LOW PITCH.
YES.
NOW YOU'RE TALKING SENSE.
AFTER SOME TIME.
YOUR UNCLE LOVES YOU. THAT IS WHY HE HAS LEFT THE BAG WITH MONEY.
© PRAN'S FEATURES

POLICE NOWHERE AROUND... PERFECT PLAN.
DON'T TRY TO ESCAPE OR I'LL SHOOT.
THAT MONEY IS MINE.
OUCH!
THUD !!
www.chachachaudhary.com

SABU UNCLE! I'D GIVEN YOUR NUMBER.
YOU DID THE RIGHT THING.
YOU HAVE INVITED YOUR DEATH.
I'LL SHOOT YOU.
OH
THUD !!
COME, LET'S GO.

Celebrating !ndia

get inspired by great personalities of India

The Great Indian Biography Series

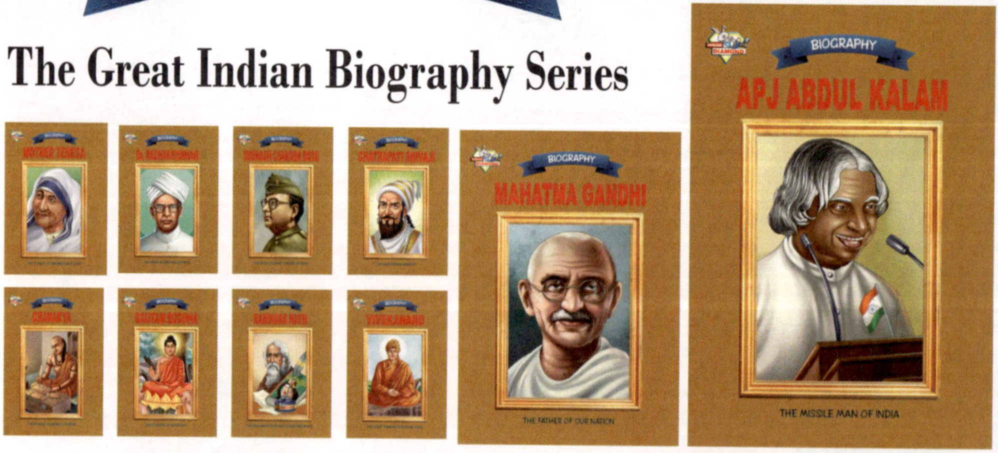

Available in Hindi, English, Bangla, Marathi & Gujarati

Order Now

JUNIOR DIAMOND

X-30, Okhla Industrial Area Phase-II, New Delhi-110020, INDIA
Tel.: 40716600 E-mail: sales@dpb.in, Website: www.dpb.in

_____ ROT

RA _____

CAB _____ E

ZUC _____ I

TO _____ O

S _____ ACH

O _____

P _____

MU _____ D

_____ KIN

PI _____ PLE

Fill in the blanks with the words BAG, CAR, CHIN, DISH, EAR, KIN, MAT, NEAP, PIN, PUMP, RANGE, STAR to reveal the names of 11 edible plants (mostly fruits and vegetables).

Fill in the blanks and send us back to win a surprise prize - write down the following details in block letter: Complete Name, Telephone Number with STD code (Mobile Number), Age, Place of Birth, Date of Birth, Gender, Email ID and Complete Postal Address with Pincode.

Discover Talent @ Diamond Toons
X-30, Okhla Industrial Area, Phase-II, New Delhi-110020
Ph.: 011-40712100, 40712200, E-mail: sales@dpb.in

Diamond TOONS
Largest selling comics in India
PRAN'S CHACHA CHAUDHARY AND SWACHH BHARAT
₹ 50 48P
Largest selling comics in India
PRAN'S BILLOO AND FISHING
₹ 50 48P
Availabe in Hindi, English, Marathi, Gujarati & Bangla
Largest selling comics in India
PRAN'S PINKI REAL WATCHMAN
₹ 50 48P
Chacha Chaudhary, Billoo & Pinki comics also available in Digest.
PRAN'S CHACHA CHAUDHARY DIGEST - 1
₹ 100 96P Size: 6.5"X9"
PRAN'S CHACHA CHAUDHARY DIGEST - 2
₹ 100 96P Size: 6.5"X9"
PRAN'S CHACHA CHAUDHARY DIGEST - 3
₹ 100 96P Size: 6.5"X9"
PRAN'S CHACHA CHAUDHARY DIGEST - 4
₹ 100 96P Size: 6.5"X9"
PRAN'S BILLOO'S DIGEST - 1
₹ 100 96P Size: 6.5"X9"
PRAN'S BILLOO'S DIGEST - 2
₹ 100 96P Size: 6.5"X9"
PRAN'S PINKI DIGEST - 1
₹ 100 96P Size: 6.5"X9"
PRAN'S PINKI DIGEST - 2
₹ 100 96P Size: 6.5"X9"
Diamond TOONS
X-30, Okhla Industrial Area Phase-II, New Delhi-110020, India
Tel.: 011-40712100, 40712200 Email: sales@dpb.in